The Things I Learn

I Learn from My Mom

Joyce Jeffries

illustrated by
Anita Morra

PowerKiDS
press.

New York

Published in 2017 by The Rosen Publishing Group, Inc.
29 East 21st Street, New York, NY 10010

Copyright © 2017 by The Rosen Publishing Group, Inc.

First Edition

Managing Editor: Nathalie Beullens-Maoui
Editor: Caitie McAneney
Book Design: Michael Flynn
Illustrator: Anita Morra

Library of Congress Cataloging-in-Publication Data

Names: Jeffries, Joyce, author.
Title: I learn from my mom / Joyce Jeffries.
Description: New York : PowerKids Press, [2017] | Series: The things I learn
Identifiers: LCCN 2015047934 | ISBN 9781499423716 (pbk.) | ISBN 9781499423730 (library bound) | ISBN 9781499423723 (6 pack)
Subjects: LCSH: Social learning–Juvenile literature. | Mothers–Juvenile
  literature.
Classification: LCC HQ783 .J43 2017 | DDC 303.3/2–dc23
LC record available at http://lccn.loc.gov/2015047934

Manufactured in the United States of America

CPSIA Compliance Information: Batch #BS16PK: For Further Information contact Rosen Publishing, New York, New York at 1-800-237-9932

Contents

My mom likes to teach me new things. We have fun learning together!

4

I learn to count with my mom.

We practice counting every day.

I learn to tie my shoes from my mom.

It's not easy!

9

My mom likes music.
She shows me how
to dance.

11

12

We learn silly dances together!

My mom and I like to play
outside. There's so much to learn!

We go to the park.

I learn the names of different
animals from my mom.

My mom teaches me how to play baseball.

My mom is a good
baseball player.

19

She teaches me how to hold a
baseball bat.

My mom knows so many things.
She's a great teacher!

Words to Know

baseball bat

park

shoes

Index

24